SPRINKLE

SHAMBLING

shambling

distinctive

giggle

luscious

Precision

dusk

Zesty

SNUG

LOZ

proclaimed

hesitated

RKLING

sway

MAY 8 2006

pulsing

encountered

oney

ambling

flippant

shu

lliftuous

RELIABLE

nuzzle

exhi

word

AMPHORA

harmony

TODDLE

tantalizing

plucked

GLORIOUS

hidden

Lyre

For Richard and Jesse,
wondrous wordsmiths/merry muses —R.S.

For Pia, collecting and saying new words every day —G.P.

Published in the United States by Schwartz & Wade Books,
an imprint of Random House Children's Books, a division of Random House, Inc., New York.

SCHWARTZ & WADE BOOKS and colophon are trademarks of Random House, Inc.

www.randomhouse.com/kids

Educators and librarians, for a variety of teaching tools, visit us at
www.randomhouse.com/teachers

Library of Congress Cataloging-in-Publication Data

Schotter, Roni.
The boy who loved words / Roni Schotter ; illustrated by Giselle Potter. — 1st ed.
        p. cm.
Summary: Selig, who loves words and copies them on pieces of paper that he carries with him,
goes on a trip to discover his purpose.
ISBN 0-375-83601-2 (alk. paper) — ISBN 0-375-93601-7 (lib. bdg.)
[1. Language and languages—Fiction. 2. Self-actualization (Psychology)—Fiction.]
I. Potter, Giselle, ill. II. Title.
PZ7.S3765 Boy 2006
[E]—dc22
2005010850

The text for this book is set in Geistserifa.
The illustrations for this book are rendered in pencil, ink, gouache, gesso, watercolor, and collage.
MANUFACTURED IN CHINA

10 9 8 7 6 5 4 3 2 1
First Edition

A NOTE ABOUT WORDSWORTH'S WONDERFUL WORDS

On the back endpapers are some of Wordsworth's wonderful words—words he loves the sound,
the taste, and the meaning of. Some of them may be new to you. If you too find them wonderful,
perhaps they may become your favorites as well. Who can tell? Maybe you'll start your
own collection of wonderful words.—R.S.

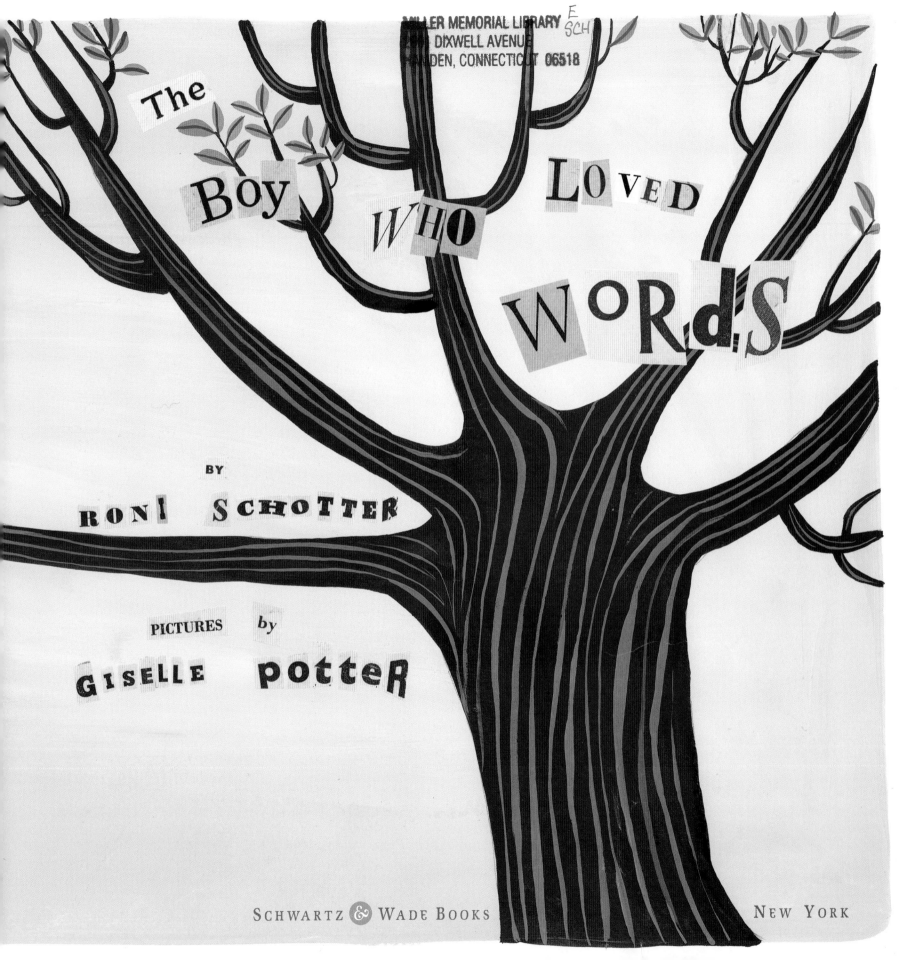

The Boy WHO LOVED WORds

BY

RONI SCHOTTER

PICTURES by

GISELLE potteR

SCHWARTZ & WADE BOOKS   NEW YORK

There are, in this world, people who are born collectors. Some collect shells or stones. Others, feathers. Some have even been known to collect tiny teaspoons. Such a one was Selig. *He* was a collector of words.

Selig loved everything about words—the sound of them in his ears (*tintinnabulating!*), the taste of them on his tongue (*tantalizing!*), the thought of them when they *percolated* in his brain (*stirring!*), and, most especially, the feel of them when they moved his heart (*Mama!*).

Whenever Selig heard a word he liked, he'd shout it loud, *jot* it down on a slip of paper, then stuff it into his pocket to save. Such a collector! Selig's pockets positively brimmed with words. He stuffed new ones inside his shirt, down his socks, up his sleeves, under his hat.

phenomenon
POROUS
smooth
Luxury
Electric
BEAUTIFUL
RARE
fragrant
Tantalize
Obligation
melted
EARNEST,
enchanted
comfortable
GENTLE
cheerful
GLEAMING-
Compliment
genuine
stirring
whisper
continuous

While other children busied themselves with bats, nets, and all manner of balls, Selig stayed on the outskirts, always on the *periphery*—listening and collecting delicious words.

His father, a practical man who sold sturdy shoes for a living, wondered
what good could possibly come from a son with such a strange *predilection*.

His mother, a large, lovely woman from the Old Country, worried—could her beautiful boy find happiness? Waving her arms in the air, she was a *windmill* of worry.

As time went on, people began calling Selig by a new name: Wordsworth. "Hey, Wordsworth," kids would *giggle*. "Here's a word for your collection—*oddball*!"

"*Oddball!*" Selig repeated. The silly-sounding word should have made him giggle, but instead it made him lonely.

One night, Selig had a dream. . . . Alone, in front of an unusual *emporium*, he *encountered* an oversized *amphora*. Curious, Selig gave it a tap. *Swooooooooosh!* Out popped a *swarthy*, *swirling* man. *"Djinn!"* Selig exclaimed, then, "Genie!" he shouted, enjoying the tang of tasty new words.

"Vhat you vant?" the Genie asked. "A vish?"

Such strange and *savory* sounds! Such an offer! At a loss for words, Selig suddenly knew his *vish*—it was for an answer. "Is it true, am I really . . . an . . . *oddball*?"

"Oddball? Feh! You are Voidsvoith, a lover of voids. Already you have vhat people search their whole life for—an enthusiasm, a *passion*. Vhat you need now is a poipose, a mission." Then, without a word of warning, the Genie disappeared.

Selig awakened from his dream. . . . *Lickety-split*, he packed a *rucksack* with a pillow and blanket, apples, honey, cream soda, and his entire collection of words. He knew exactly what he had to do. Selig took to the road, determined to find his purpose.

silky, rigid EMPORIUM velvet,

On the trail of his purpose, Selig's senses sharpened. He noted the nod and *toddle* of tulips in the wind; the sway and *swagger* of tree branches; how, at evening, the light dimmed to announce the arrival of twilight and stars. *Dusk*, Selig noted, adding that short and enchanting word to his collection.

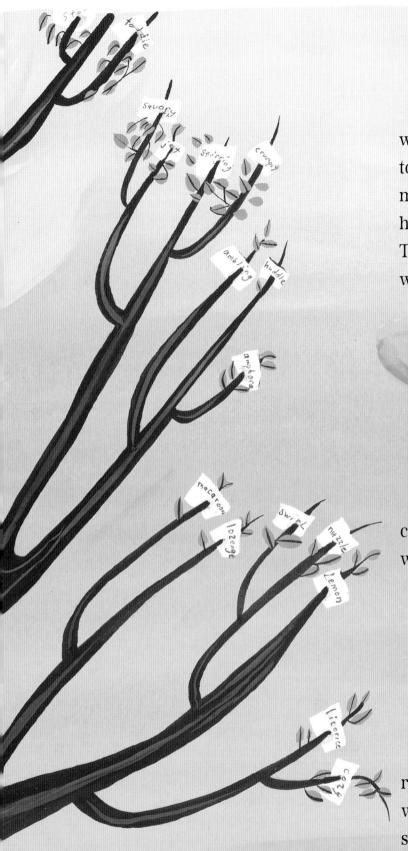

But in time Selig's step grew heavy. Under the weight of so many words, it was harder and harder to move. He was *shuffling* and *shambling* when he might have been *rambling* and *ambling*. Perhaps what he needed to do was lighten his load. But HOW? Throw words away? Waste them? Impossible! They were far too precious!

Selig was too tired to think. His exhausted brain could imagine but one thing—*slumber*, a splendid word! Sadly, he was too sleepy to write it down.

In front of Selig stood a large and lovely tree. He removed his jacket, stuffed, like his mama's *strudel*, with words. Tenderly, he hung each word on its own separate branch, as if putting it to bed for the night.

With a sip of cream soda and a nibble of honeyed apple, Selig *clambered*, then curled in a *crook* of the tree. *Snug*, he thought, and fell directly to sleep. Comfortably cradled there, he dreamed of his mama, his mission, and *macaroons*—his favorite cookie.

During the night, a pacing poet, unable to sleep for want of a word, found himself under the same tree, gazing hopelessly at the moon. Night after night, he'd been struggling to find the right words to describe it.

Suddenly, mysteriously, a swirling wind blew up. Four of Selig's words sailed off their branches. Reaching skyward, the distracted poet caught them. Discarding the word *macaroon*, he held tightly to *lozenge, lemon,* and *licorice.* "The moon," he wrote in his notebook, growing more and more excited with each word, "melted like a *lemon lozenge* in the *licorice* sky."

"My stars!" the poet shouted, *exvltant.* "That's it!"

The following morning Selig awoke to what could only be called a *rhapsody* of birds and words. The poet was reading his newest poem aloud—a poem *chockablock* with Selig's words!

the MOON melted like a lemon lozenge in the LICORICE sky

rhapsodizing

Wiping the sleep crumbs from his eyes, Selig scrambled down the tree and saluted the poet. "Your poem," he told him, "contains some of my favorite words. How beautifully you use them."

"Why, thank you. For once, the words just seemed to come to me. Upon my word! How lucky I am! What, may I ask, is your name? I should like to dedicate my poem to you."

For a moment, Selig *hesitated*. Then, suddenly, for the first time ever, he proudly *proclaimed*, "They call me Wordsworth."

It was then that Selig realized his mission. It was spreading the word—sharing his words with others!

From that day forth, Selig's steps were light and filled with purpose. Ever the collector, he added new words as it pleased him. But now, whenever he felt word-heavy, he discovered the ideal places to *sprinkle*, *disburse*, and *broadcast* them.

In that way, a baker whose pastries had always been ignored found his shop filled with a mob of hungry customers. When the baker's back was turned, Selig, on a macaroon break, had tossed some of his favorite words into the air. *Crispy* and *crunchy* landed next to the crumpets. *Scrumptious* fell against a loaf of pumpernickel. *Luscious* leaned against a layer cake. "Upon my word! How lucky I am!" the baker exclaimed when he turned back and saw his *voracious* new customers.

Neighbors realized they were bickering when the words *fuss, hubbub,* and *jibber-jabber* rained down on them . . . and stopped their fighting.

Selig watched them grow still and gaze kindly upon one another after
he cast *hush*, *harmony*, and *chum* in their direction.

And so, by word of mouth, the legend began. . . . "It's Wordsworth," people would whisper, when, suddenly, the right word occurred to them. "HE is near," they would nod, knowingly. "Upon my word! How lucky we are!"

Years passed. Selig was a man now, also a *myth*. But while he delighted in his work, he found that, once again, he was lonely. "*Solo*," he sighed.

One day, after launching the words *limber*, *spry*, and *gusto* toward an aging, unhappy man, Selig heard a sound on the breeze. A single, *pulsing*, marvelous note floated through the air and found its way straight into his heart. *"Mellifluous!"* he exclaimed.

Pursuing that perfect note, Selig found a young woman seated by a lake, playing a *lute*. Suddenly, his heart was *aflutter. Tremulously* he asked, "M-m-may I have a word with you? Wh-wh-what is your name?"

"They call me Melody," the woman sang out. The music of her voice, combined with the charm of her words, was, to Selig, the sweetest of all songs.

It was love at first listen. Together, they journeyed back to Selig's hometown, to his mother and father. What a reunion! How his mother smiled when she saw them! Worried that they looked thin, she cooked Selig's favorite foods—brisket, dumplings, plum crumble, *strudel*, and, of course, macaroons. To comfort their tired feet, Selig's father *cobbled* the couple his sturdiest shoes.

Rested and restored, Selig resumed his life's work, joyfully gathering and scattering words on the wind. Since then, word by word, *legions* of lucky people have discovered and delighted in them.

You too may find yourself lucky if, one day, while you are thinking or writing or simply speaking, the perfect word just seems to come to you. If so, you'll know that Selig is near. And on special days, if you feel like humming or suddenly bursting into song, you'll know that Melody is with him. "Upon my word!" you may say. "How lucky I am!"

GLOSSARY
(IN ALPHABETICAL ORDER)

AFLUTTER—beating quickly

AMBLING—walking easily

AMPHORA—two-handled vase

BROADCAST—to spread widely over an area

CHOCKABLOCK—crowded

CHUM—friend, pal

CLAMBERED—climbed with hands and feet

COBBLED—put together

CRISPY—firm, fresh, easy to crumble

CROOK—a bend or curve

CRUNCHY—crackling fresh

DISBURSE—to distribute, pass out

DJINN—genie, magical person who grants wishes

DUSK—dark part of twilight

EMPORIUM—large store

ENCOUNTERED—met

EXULTANT—full of joy

FUSS—unneeded excitement

GIGGLE—to laugh in a silly way

GUSTO—great enjoyment

HARMONY—a feeling of agreement

HESITATED—waited because of being unsure

HUBBUB—loud, mixed-up noise

HUSH—be quiet

JIBBER-JABBER—nonsense talk

JOT—to write quickly

LEGIONS—large numbers

LEMON—yellow, like the fruit

LICKETY-SPLIT—very fast, right away

LICORICE—black, like the candy

LIMBER—able to bend easily

LOZENGE—small candy, sometimes with medicine in it

LUSCIOUS—rich and delicious

LUTE—a guitar-like musical instrument

STRUDEL

GUSTO

spry

comfort

ACC

CROOK

handy

COBBLED

SLUMBER

stimulate

solo

ODDBALL

ted

WINDMILL

rious

liveliness